Ranger's Pledge

I give my pledge as a member of
Ranger Rick's Nature Club

To use my eyes to see the
beauty of all outdoors;

To train my mind to learn
the importance of nature;

To use my hands to protect our air,
soil, water, woods and wildlife;

And by good example, to show
others how to respect,
properly use, and enjoy
our natural resources.

_____
Ranger's Name

Library of Congress Cataloging-in-Publication Data

Boyle, Doe.

Rick's First Adventure / adapted by Doe Boyle ; illustrated by Alton Langford.
    p.   cm. — (Adventures of Ranger Rick)
"From an original article which appeared in *Ranger Rick* magazine,
© National Wildlife Federation"

Summary: Ranger Rick Raccoon reminisces with his animal friends about
the day they saved Shady Pond from trash and pollutants and decided to
form Ranger Rick's Nature Club to guard and protect wild and beautiful
places forever.
    ISBN 0-924483-45-8
[1. Pollution — Fiction. 2. Environmental protection — Fiction.
3. Raccoons — Fiction. 4. Animals — Fiction.] I. Langford, Alton, ill.
II. Ranger Rick. III. Title. IV. Series
    PZ7.B69647Ri   1992
    [E]—dc20
                            92-11868
                             AC

Adventures of
Ranger Rick®

Rick's First Adventure

Adapted by Doe Boyle • Illustrated by Alton Langford

A Division of Trudy Management Corporation
Norwalk, Connecticut

A bitter wind rattled the branches of Ranger Rick Raccoon's hollow oak tree home in Deep Green Wood. Rick, Scarlett Fox, Ollie Otter, and Punky Porcupine snuggled together in Rick's cozy den, waiting for the snowstorm to stop. To pass the time, they told jokes and stories, giggling and gasping over the happy and exciting adventures they had shared.

"Tell us the story of the time you saved Benny Bass, Rick," Scarlett Fox urged.

"Oh, that's a fine story," Rick remembered. "It was the very first adventure of the animal team in Deep Green Wood."

"Tell it! Tell it!" the others encouraged. So Rick began...

"Late in spring many years ago, Ollie, Becky Hare, and I decided to go down to Shady Pond one beautiful afternoon to visit Benny. We hadn't been there in months, and we were eager to see Benny. Ollie raced ahead down the path and dived into the pond. Suddenly he let out a yell.

"'Something terrible has happened,' he shouted.

"When we reached the edge of the pond, we saw an awful mess. Cans and bottles and paper and plastic trash littered the bare ground around the pond, and muddy gullies creased the bank where rainwater had washed away the soil. The water was muddy and splotched with greasy globs of oil, and Benny swam close to the surface, looking sick.

"'Benny!' I cried. 'What has happened to Shady Pond?'

"Poor Benny choked out a terrible tale. 'It started last winter,' he said. 'People came here to ice skate and threw their picnic trash everywhere. In the spring other people came by and dumped old tires and oil cans into the water. When summer came, campers arrived and trampled the grass and damaged the bushes along the banks until nothing was left but bare ground. Now the rain washes mud into the pond, and the water is so dirty I can hardly breathe!'

"When we heard that," Rick continued, "we were sad for Benny and angry about the carelessness of the people who nearly ruined our favorite swimming place. Right then and there, I saw that the animals had to join together to save Shady Pond and all of Deep Green Wood.

"'Round up the other animals,' I said to my friends. 'We're going to clean this mess up.'

"Soon Sammy Squirrel, Chester Chipmunk, Odora Skunk, Molly Muskrat, and many others joined us. 'All right, gang — let's get to work!' I told them. 'Sammy and Chester, you twist some vines into strong ropes — we'll need them to pull the tires out of the pond. Ollie, you dive for oil cans and other trash. Odora, you and I will pick up bottles and cans and sort them into piles to take to the recycling center. Zelda Possum and Cubby Bear, you gather rocks and fill up those muddy gullies. Molly and Becky, you pack dry leaves and grass along the sides of the gullies so the rain can't wash the mud into the pond.'

"We worked for hours and finally the job was done. Tired but proud, we admired Shady Pond. 'It will take time for the water to clear,' I told the animals, 'but Shady Pond sure looks a lot better.'

"'Thanks to all of you,' Benny added.

"'But what happens the next time people mess it up?' Ollie asked sadly.

"'We'll just have to see that they don't,' I answered. 'We'll work to keep the water clean and clear.'

"'I have an idea,' Becky cried. 'We became a great team to do this job. Let's stay a team, with Rick as our leader! Let's call ourselves *Rick's Rangers*!'

"All the animals cheered and shouted their agreement. 'Rick's our leader,' yelled Becky. 'We're his team!' said Cubby. 'We'll guard wild and beautiful places forever!' added Zelda.

"And that, everybody, is how Rick's Rangers came to be," Rick finished proudly.

"Wow!" Punky said. "So *that* was the beginning! And now Scarlett handles the job with you!"

"Right — I couldn't do it without her as a partner," Rick agreed. "And I couldn't do it without you and all the other Rangers around the world. Now hundreds of thousands of Rangers are busy recycling, fighting pollution, and helping wild creatures everywhere. Each of us promises to help change the world for the better every time we say the Ranger's pledge."

"Let's say it now, Rick!" suggested Ollie.

"Sure," said Rick. "Any time is a good time to renew the Ranger's most important promise."

Punky, Ollie, and Scarlett raised their right paws and joined Rick in a cheerful recital of the Ranger's pledge.

I give my pledge as a member of Ranger Rick's Nature Club
To use my eyes to see the beauty of all outdoors;
To train my mind to learn the importance of nature;
To use my hands to protect our air, soil, water, woods, and wildlife;
And by my good example, to show others how to respect,
   properly use, and enjoy our natural resources.

Smiling proudly, the animals crowded around the hole of Rick's hollow-tree home and admired the sparkling clean snow in their beautiful Deep Green Wood.